Books by Bruce Coville

The A.I. Gang Trilogy
Operation Sherlock
Robot Trouble
Forever Begins Tomorrow

Bruce Coville's Alien Adventures
Aliens Ate My Homework
I Left My Sneakers in Dimension X
The Search for Snout

Camp Haunted Hills
How I Survived My Summer Vacation
Some of My Best Friends Are Monsters
The Dinosaur that Followed Me Home

Magic Shop Books
Jennifer Murdley's Toad
Jeremy Thatcher, Dragon Hatcher
The Monster's Ring

My Teacher Books
My Teacher Is an Alien
My Teacher Fried My Brains
My Teacher Glows in the Dark
My Teacher Flunked the Planet

Space Brat Books
Space Brat
Space Brat 2: Blork's Evil Twin
Space Brat 3: The Wrath of Squat
Space Brat 4: Planet of the Dips

The Dragonslayers
Goblins in the Castle
Monster of the Year

Available from MINSTREL Books

BRUCE COVILLE

The World's Worst Fairy Godmother

Illustrated by
Katherine Coville

BIRCH GROVE
Hazel Widlund Media Center
Independent School District No. 279
Osseo, Minnesota

A MINSTREL® HARDCOVER
PUBLISHED BY POCKET BOOKS
New York London Toronto Sydney Tokyo Singapore

A MINSTREL HARDCOVER

 A Minstrel Book published by
POCKET BOOKS, a division of Simon & Schuster Inc.
1230 Avenue of the Americas, New York, NY 10020

ISBN: 0-671-00229-5

First Minstrel Books hardcover printing January 1997

10 9 8 7 6 5 4 3 2 1

A MINSTREL BOOK and colophon are registered trademarks
of Simon & Schuster Inc.

Printed in the U.S.A.

For Barbara Russell,

who helped bring this story to life by waving her magic wand over it the first time it was presented on stage

Contents

Chapter 1

Another Fine Mess

Maybelle Clodnowski stood at the edge of the swamp and took two frogs from her apron pocket.

"Here we go," she said, looking at them fondly. "This should suit you just fine."

Before Maybelle could put the frogs into the water she heard someone clear his throat behind her. It was a deep sound. A fierce sound. A definitely disapproving sound.

Maybelle turned around. Her eyes went wide. She swallowed once, then whispered, "Hello, boss."

Mr. Peters was as tall and slender as Maybelle was short and podgy. His nostrils flared, and he raised his eyebrows so high Maybelle

was afraid they might shoot right over the top of his forehead and keep on going.

"What," he asked in his deepest, crankiest, most boy-are-you-in-trouble-now voice, "what in heaven's name do you think you're doing?"

"Sending the young lovers off to a new life?" asked Maybelle, smiling hopefully.

Mr. Peters scowled.

"They're both happy," Maybelle added defensively.

"Happy?" roared Mr. Peters. "*Happy!* Maybelle, they're both *frogs!*"

"Well, they like the outdoors."

Mr. Peters made a rumbling sound deep in his chest. "Maybelle, the prince of Burundia and the princess of Ghukistan were not raised to be frogs. They were raised to be rulers of a kingdom."

"Well, I know that, boss. But the poor things really didn't like the idea much, and I was trying—"

"You *were* trying, you *are* trying, and it looks very much as if you always *will be* trying!" roared Mr. Peters. He made a gesture with his hands, and the frogs disappeared. In their place, coughing and wheezing in a cloud of blue smoke, stood a handsome prince and an extremely beautiful princess. Both looked bewildered and a little embarrassed.

"You two go on home," said Mr. Peters sharply. "As for you, Maybelle, I want you to meet me in my office tomorrow morning at nine sharp."

With another wave of his hand he disappeared in a cloud of white smoke.

The smell of newly mown hay lingered behind him.

"His office?" asked the prince, stepping out of the swamp. He shook a minnow from his boot.

"Up there," said Maybelle, pointed toward the sky.

"Heaven?" asked the princess, her blue eyes wide.

"You could call it that," said Maybelle. "Though at the moment it doesn't quite feel that way." She sighed, then turned her eyes from the clouds back to the swamp. "I'm terribly sorry about the frog thing. I didn't mean for it to happen that way. When Princess Igrella kissed you, Prince Arbus, you were supposed to turn back into a human. Why Princess Igrella turned into a frog instead I'll never know."

She shook her wand in disgust, then tucked

it into the belt that held her skirt close to her plump waist.

Princess Igrella patted Maybelle on the shoulder. "No need to apologize. I was pretty upset at first, but when I thought about life in court versus life in the swamp . . . well, somehow a lily pad began to seem a lot more comfortable than a throne. As far as I'm concerned, all that really mattered was that Prince Arbus and I could be together."

Maybelle smiled. "At least you're still both the same species. But maybe I can—"

Prince Arbus put his arm around Igrella's tiny waist. "We'll be fine, Maybelle," he said nobly. "One way or another. Please . . . feel free to go on to your next case."

"But maybe I should stay and—"

"We'll be fine," the prince repeated firmly, his voice a little desperate. "Thank you for your help."

"Oh, it was my pleasure," said Maybelle cheerfully. She glanced at the sky. "Certainly more of a pleasure than tomorrow morning is going to be."

The cloud directly above her grew dark and rumbled with thunder.

5

Maybelle rolled her eyes. "Such a fuss over one little mistake."

A bolt of lightning seared down beside her, charring a clump of ferns just inches from her right foot.

"All right, all right! So it wasn't a *little* mistake. So no one's perfect, all right? I'll see you in the morning."

Wrapping her cloak around her, Maybelle vanished in a cloud of pink smoke.

The smell of fresh-baked muffins lingered behind her.

"I hope she'll be all right," whispered Princess Igrella.

"I'm sure Maybelle will be fine," said the prince. "It's her next client that I'm worried about." He shook his head. "Really, she has to be the worst fairy godmother in the entire world."

As Prince Arbus guided Princess Igrella out of the swamp, a teardrop fell from far above him, landing on his head.

Chapter 2

Maybelle's Last Chance

The next morning Maybelle hurried across heaven, leaping from cloud to cloud, trying not to get sunshine on her feet. The angels watched in amusement. The cherubs were in a state of high hysteria.

"Late again," she muttered, missing a cloud and falling several feet before her wings could catch her. "Late again. Oh, Mr. Peters is going to be mad, mad, mad."

Maybelle was almost, but not totally, correct. Mr. Peters was not merely mad. He was furious.

"Maybelle, can't you do anything right?" he exploded, when she reached the spacious cloud where he had his office.

7

"Of course I can, boss!"

"All right, name one thing," he replied, crossing his arms. "One single thing that you've done right in the last one hundred and fifty-three years."

Maybelle paused. She started to speak, then shook her head. She made a face. She started to speak again, then sighed. Suddenly her eyes lit up. "How about that lovely gown I wove for Princess Aurora? The one I made of cobwebs and eiderdown and stitched together with moonbeams?"

"It was beautiful," agreed Mr. Peters. "Until it started to rain and the gown dissolved—*while* she was wearing it!"

Maybelle hunched into herself. "So I made a little slip."

"You made a *very* little slip!" roared Mr. Peters. "That's why the princess was so embarrassed!" He shook his head and took a deep breath. "I'm sorry. I shouldn't lose my temper that way. I would have been promoted by now if I could break the habit. But really, Maybelle, you're the only one who does that to me. I never even raise my voice to anyone except you. What am I going to do with you?"

Before Maybelle could answer, he said,

"Never mind. I'll tell you what I'm going to do. I'm going to give you another chance. Your last chance."

Maybelle gulped. *"Last* chance?" she asked nervously.

Mr. Peters nodded. "This is it. Either you pull this one off, or you can trade in your wings and your wand for good."

"Mr. Peters, you can't do that to me! The only thing I ever wanted to be is a fairy godmother!"

"Well, I hope you've got a second choice in mind."

"But you can't—"

"Maybelle, you've had well over a century to get this right! As far as I can tell, you're no better at it now than when you started. I'm sorry, but I can't let this go on forever. I've already given you more chances than I should have. I'm starting to get complaints from upstairs." He rolled his eyes, indicating the next level of clouds above them. In a whisper he said, "I had to pull strings just to get this job for you. So to make sure nothing goes wrong, you're going to have a supervisor."

"A supervisor? Jeepers, boss, what do you think I am? An amateur?"

9

"Yes. Now, your supervisor will be along simply to make sure things don't get too far out of hand. This is still your job. She will step in only if you muff things. But if she *does* have to step in . . ." He scowled and made a gesture with his hands. It looked as if he was breaking something in half.

Maybelle clutched her wand. "You wouldn't!"

"Yes," said Mr. Peters, "I would."

Maybelle sighed. "Who is this supervisor?"

"Edna Prim."

"Not *the* Edna Prim?" cried Maybelle, her eyes growing wide.

Mr. Peters nodded.

"Fairy Godmother of the Year for the last hundred and forty-seven years running? *That* Edna Prim?"

"The same."

"She's my hero!"

As Maybelle spoke, a tall, stern-looking woman floated down to the cloud. Her dress billowed charmingly around her. "Good morning, Mr. Peters," she said. "I came as soon as I could."

"There it is!" cried Maybelle, rushing forward. "The Fairy Godmother of the Year medallion! Oh, I am so impressed."

She clutched the medallion, pulling Edna's neck forward as she did. "It's beautiful," gasped Maybelle.

"Yes, it is, isn't it?" said Edna, yanking it back. She shook herself, looking something like a tall, thin cat that has just heard a joke of which it faintly disapproved.

"You understand the assignment, Edna?" asked Mr. Peters.

Edna nodded. "It seems like a fairly simple case. I don't see how anyone could mess it up."

"You'd be surprised," said Mr. Peters darkly.

"Wait a minute," said Maybelle. "I don't understand. What *is* the assignment?"

"You'll see when we get there," said Mr. Peters. "In fact, if you're both ready, I think we should be leaving. Just follow me, ladies. . . ."

With a wave of his hand, he disappeared.

Edna vanished a second later, leaving the scent of heavily starched laundry lingering in the air behind her.

"Wait for me!" cried Maybelle. Rushing forward, she leaped off the cloud and hurtled toward the earth far below.

She was halfway down before she remembered the spell for following the others.

Chapter 3

Little Miss Perfect

Mr. Peters and Edna were waiting beside a small, tidy-looking building that stood at the edge of a small, tidy-looking town named Grindersnog. They were invisible to human eyes.

"For heaven's sake, Maybelle, hide yourself," snapped Mr. Peters when Maybelle floated down beside them.

Maybelle sighed. Then she muttered a few words as she made a circle over her head with her wand. She disappeared instantly—except for her left foot. It looked very strange standing there all by itself.

"Drat!" she muttered. Reaching down, she tapped her foot several times with her wand. Finally the foot disappeared too.

Edna rolled her eyes but said nothing.

"All right," said Mr. Peters. "It's time to meet your next client, Maybelle. Let's slip inside."

Following Mr. Peters and Edna through a crack in the door, Maybelle found herself standing at the back of a schoolroom. Standing at the front of the room was a very harried-looking teacher.

About twenty children sat on hard wooden benches, working on slates. For about two minutes everyone was very quiet. Then a boy near the front of the room took a large spider from his pocket.

Maybelle giggled when she realized that the spider was made of black paper.

Edna poked her in the ribs.

Using a string attached to one end, the boy dangled the spider over the shoulder of the girl in front of him.

The girl leaped to her feet. "Teacher! Teacher!" she shrieked.

The teacher sighed. "What is it, Maria?"

By now Maria had figured out that the spider was made of paper. Straightening her shoulders, she said with great dignity, "Gustav *tried* to scare me."

"Well, I think he succeeded," replied the teacher. "Gustav, you will stay after school today."

"Yes, Herr Bauer," replied Gustav with a sigh.

"Ah, I see," Maybelle whispered to Mr. Peters. "You want me to work with Gustav."

"No. Keep watching."

Two rows ahead of them a dark-haired boy reached forward and pinched a girl who had long braids. She immediately turned and punched him in the nose. He jumped to his feet, howling with anger. But before he could hit her back, the teacher snapped. "Friedrich! Heidi! What is this all about?"

"He pinched me!" cried Heidi.

"She *punched* me!" whined Friedrich.

"You did it first!"

"Did not!"

"Did too!"

"Did not!"

"Enough!" bellowed Herr Bauer. "If you twins can't get along, I'll have to separate you."

"Good!" cried both of them together.

"I will also have to inform your parents of that fact," the teacher said ominously.

The twins sank into their seats, muttering unhappily.

"Ah, it's *them*," said Maybelle. "Well, twins really ought to be able to get along. I think I can—"

"Keep watching," said Mr. Peters.

A boy in the third row began to smile. Taking something from his pocket, he poked the shoulder of the girl in front of him. When she turned, he held up a huge earthworm and mouthed the word "Watch."

Then he popped the worm into his mouth and swallowed it.

"Teacher!" shrieked the girl. "Ludwig ate a . . . a *worm!*"

"Me?" asked Ludwig, his face full of puzzled innocence.

"I saw you!" cried the girl.

"Do you have any evidence?" asked Ludwig.

"Of course not. You *swallowed* it!"

Herr Bauer had been watching this with one hand pressed to his forehead, as if he had a throbbing headache. Now he said, "All right, that's enough. Helga, calm down. Ludwig, save your lunch for recess."

"Oh, yuck!" cried Maybelle. "Are you going to give me that horrible Ludwig for a client?"

Mr. Peters shook his head.

"But Helga doesn't need—"

"It's not her, either."

"Oh, I've got it!" said Maybelle happily. "It's Herr Bauer! That makes sense. With a class like this, he needs some help."

"No, Maybelle. It's not the teacher."

"But . . ."

"Keep watching."

Now a girl who had been sitting quietly in the front row stood up. She had blond hair and bright blue eyes. She was quite pretty, and her dress was so clean and perfect it looked as if it had just been made that morning.

Her posture was flawless.

Walking to the teacher's desk, she placed her slate on it as if delivering a gift from the gods. Then she stood beside the desk, something almost like a smirk on her face, as the teacher examined her work.

"Susan, this work is wonderful—as usual."

"Thank you," replied Susan. "I tried my best—as usual."

Three of the boys began to cough.

Susan flounced back to her bench.

"*That's* your client," said Mr. Peters.

17

"Susan?" Maybelle asked in astonishment. "But why? She's already just about perfect."

"Precisely."

"But all those other little monsters—"

"Are perfectly normal children—sometimes nice, sometimes disgusting. No, Susan is your case."

"But what's wrong with her?"

"Susan Pfenstermacher is a wonderful child. Unfortunately, she *thinks* she's perfect."

Maybelle's eyes went wide. "Uh-oh," she whispered.

"Precisely," said Mr. Peters.

Outside the schoolhouse a small red creature who had been peeking through the window did a little jig and chuckled with devilish glee.

"Wait till I tell the boss about this!" he cried.

Chapter 4

Little Stinkers

The creature who had been listening at the window was an imp named Zitzel. He had been sent to spy on Maybelle, and as soon as he heard her assignment he gave a wicked little chuckle and scurried away.

Zitzel was about two feet tall. He was a hundred and seventeen years old—very young for an imp. He had red skin, tiny nubs of horns growing out of his forehead, and a long tail. A stubby pair of batlike wings sprouted from his shoulders.

Zitzel loved mischief more than anything. On his way out of town he managed to startle three old ladies, frighten a cat, and make the glassblower sneeze at the worst possible moment.

He was very pleased with himself.

When Zitzel entered the forest, he began to travel with more caution. The forest was scary—even for an imp. The trees were gnarled and twisty, with branches like the fingers of witches and trunks that were often as big around as a house. Sometimes, late at night, he thought they moved on their own—though he was never able to catch them at it.

Zitzel had gone only a little way into the forest when he spotted a woodcutter coming toward him, carrying a bundle of sticks on his back. The little imp wasn't sure what to do. His boss had told him not to let anyone see him. But it was already too late for that.

Well, he decided, *since I've already been spotted, I might as well have some fun.*

Making a horrible face, Zitzel ran straight at the woodcutter, waving his arms, rolling his eyes, and shouting, "Ackety-backety-backety-backety!" (He made up the words on the spot, in honor of the occasion.)

The poor man dropped his load of wood and ran screaming in the other direction.

Humming contentedly, Zitzel continued toward the cave that he shared with his boss.

He couldn't wait to tell Zozmagog what he had learned about Maybelle.

Zitzel's destination lay deep in the forest, in the side of a rocky hill. Though the opening was small, the cave itself was large and roomy. A clear stream ran through the cave's back section. Near the center of the cave, on a large stone, sat a glass ball the size of a large pumpkin. The ball flickered with red light. The light was dim, barely enough to let someone with good eyes make his way across the cave. But it cast eerie shadows that pleased the cave's occupants, who could see in the dark anyway.

In the back of the cave sat Zozmagog. He was muttering to himself in a cranky fashion. He was cranky for many reasons, some of them well over a hundred years old, some of them things he still hadn't thought of yet. Right now he was especially cranky for three reasons. First, he was having problems with his tail again, and it made his bottom hurt. Second, he had just decided that he didn't like the fact that the sky was blue. Third, his assistant was taking too long to get back with the news he wanted.

Zozmagog sighed, a hot, steamy sigh it had

taken him nearly thirty years of practice to learn to do properly. (That had been a hundred years ago, but the memory of it still made him cranky.) He was thinking about going outside to turn a bird into a stone, which always made him feel better, when he heard a shout from the front of the cave.

"Boss! Boss! I got it!"

"Got what, you twit?"

"Maybelle's next assignment!"

Zozmagog's face lit up as if he had just been told he could have a thousand pounds of itching powder at half price. Hurrying to the front of the cave (the back was his private area), he said, "Good work, Zitzel! Who is it?"

The little imp who stood at the front of the cave was bouncing up and down with excitement. "It's no one you've ever heard of." He chuckled. "I guess after that frogifying stunt we pulled with the prince of Burundia they're not going to trust Maybelle with any more royalty."

Zozmagog smiled at the memory, then quickly became very businesslike. "All right, tell me about this peasant."

"Her name is Susan Pfenstermacher. She

lives in the village at the edge of the forest,
just like your source told you she would."

Zozmagog nodded. "Good. Now, what's her
problem?"

"She's too good."

"What?"

"She's too good."

"That doesn't make any sense," said Zozmagog. He gave Zitzel a noogie between his
stubby horns.

"Ow! Cut that out, boss. Anyway, you'd understand if you saw her. She flounces around
like she was you-know-who's gift to the world.
I bet everyone who meets her wants to slap
her."

Zozmagog's eyes lit up. "Aha! I think I've
got the picture. Good work, Zitzel. Now, you
weren't seen, were you?"

Zitzel looked uncomfortable.

"Zitzel . . . ?"

The smaller imp still didn't answer. Zozmagog reached out and snatched his tail.

"No boss! No, don't!" cried Zitzel. But it was
too late. Zozmagog began to twist.

"I asked if anybody saw you."

"Ow! Ow-ow-*ow!* Yes, someone saw me. But
only for a minute!"

Zozmagog let go of Zitzel's tail. "You idiot! I told you not to let yourself be seen! Who was it?"

"Just some woodcutter at the edge of the forest."

"Stay out of my sight!" snapped Zozmagog. "Stay out of everyone's sight while you're at it!"

Chuckling to himself, Zitzel scampered into the cave. His tail didn't really hurt—he just yelled like that when Zozmagog twisted it because it seemed to make the boss happy. Zitzel had never been able to figure out why Zozmagog thought tails were sensitive; his own never hurt at all. The boss sure was weird for an imp. But he was great at thinking up new mischief, and that was what really counted.

Zozmagog stood outside the cave, tapping his chin with his finger and muttering to himself. "Ever since I put that hex on Maybelle's wand, she's made one mess after another. That frog episode was the worst one yet. I'll bet this Pfenstermacher kid is her last chance. If I can mess Maybelle up just one more time it ought to end that wretched little fairy godmother's career forever! Ha! Aha! Ah-ha-ha-ha-ha-ha!"

His laughter peeled the bark off a nearby sapling, startling a squirrel that happened to be bouncing past. The squirrel had an acorn in its mouth. Zozmagog turned the acorn into a brick, just because he was in such a good mood.

Still laughing, he turned and skipped back into the cave.

Chapter 5

Maybelle's Plan

The next morning two women entered the little village of Grindersnog. One was tall and thin, the other short and plump. Standing side by side, they looked like the letter *b*.

From head to toe they were dressed just like any of the village women. The short one, however, had a tendency to float a bit and was having a hard time keeping her feet on the ground.

"Edna, do we really have to do this?" she asked, sounding slightly grumpy. "These shoes are killing me!"

"Tut-tut, Maybelle," said her tall companion in a prim voice. "A little discomfort is a small price to pay for a chance to observe your client in a natural setting. After all, how can you help Susan without knowing more about her?"

"Easy! I just wiggle my wand a bit. Here a poof, there a poof, everywhere a poof-poof. Presto change-o, you've got—"

"Instant disaster," said Edna darkly.

"Well, I miss my wings."

"Wings are a minor part of our job. Ah, look—there's Susan's house. Let's watch."

The two women stood beneath a tree. Without ever actually seeming to disappear, Edna slowly became invisible. Maybelle turned invisible too. But in her case, she vanished in a shower of sparks and with a distinct *pop!*

"For heaven's sake, Maybelle," whispered Edna sharply.

"Sorry," said Maybelle, who was just happy that she no longer had to keep her feet on the ground.

They waited in silence, except for once when Maybelle sneezed.

After about ten minutes Susan came out of her house. Her golden hair was wrapped around her head in a braid from which not a single strand escaped. Her spotless white dress was perfectly pressed. "Good-bye, Mother!" she called in a voice that sounded like honey and sunshine. "I'll see you this afternoon. I love you!"

"Good-bye, dear," replied a tired-looking woman. She was leaning against the doorframe, and her eyes were bleary with exhaustion. "You look lovely."

"Thank you, Mother dearest!"

The truth was, Susan had been looking lovely for more than an hour. She had refused to leave for school, however, until she thought she looked *perfect*.

Mornings were never easy at the Pfenstermacher house.

As Maybelle and Edna watched, Susan walked slowly along the cobbled streets of the little village—past the bakery, past the candlemaker's shop, past the house where Dr. Derek Dekter lived and worked. Though other children were on their way to school as well, Susan did not walk with them. And none of them called out to her to join them.

In fact, they seemed to go out of their way to avoid her.

Near the church sat a blind beggar. He was holding a tin cup in front of him. Flouncing up to the beggar, Susan looked around. She waited until the woman who was sweeping her front step on the other side of the street glanced up, then pulled a coin from her pocket. "Oh, gracious!" she cried dramatically. "A poor blind beggar. I must help the dear man!"

Smiling, Susan threw the coin into the beggar's cup with such force that the clink could be heard up and down the street.

"There," she said loudly. "That's good." Looking upward, she added piously, "After all,

we must ever be mindful of those less fortunate than ourselves."

The woman across the street rolled her eyes. With a snort, she went back into the house and slammed the door.

For just an instant Susan let her shoulders slump. Then she straightened her back so that her posture was once again perfect and continued toward school.

"Why did that woman give Susan such a nasty look?" whispered Maybelle.

Edna sighed. "Really, Maybelle. Sometimes I think you're hopeless."

"But Susan did a good thing."

"Susan only gave that beggar some money to make herself look good."

"*No!*" cried Maybelle in astonishment.

"Yes. Now come along. We need to have a little chat with Susan's mother."

Mrs. Pfenstermacher had already gone back into her house. This did not stop Edna, who simply marched up to the door and knocked firmly three times. She counted to six, then quickly stepped aside, so that when the door opened, a slightly surprised Maybelle found herself facing Mrs. Pfenstermacher.

Looking past the frazzled woman, Maybelle could see that the house was considerably tidier than most places in heaven.

"Yes?" asked the woman.

"Uh . . ." said Maybelle, painfully aware that Edna would be listening to whatever she said. "Uh . . ."

Edna poked her.

"Uh . . . it's about your daughter."

Mrs. Pfenstermacher looked suspicious. "What about her?"

"Um, she's very . . . she's very . . . *nice!*"

Mrs. Pfenstermacher's eyes widened. "Do you really think so?" she asked. She sounded quite surprised.

Maybelle felt as surprised as Mrs. Pfenstermacher looked. "Well, yes, I guess so." She paused, then asked, "Don't *you?*"

"Oh, of course!" said Mrs. Pfenstermacher quickly. "But something about Susan seems to . . . well, to upset people."

"In what way?" asked Maybelle.

Mrs. Pfenstermacher looked sad. "Well, she doesn't seem to have any friends. In fact, most of the time the other girls won't play with her at all." She paused. "They did have a game called 'Dead Girl' that they let her play last year. Susan always had to be the dead one." Mrs. Pfenstermacher sighed. "She said that was because she was the one most likely to become an angel."

"I see," said Maybelle.

A little tear trickled down Mrs. Pfenstermacher's cheek. "My own mother won't talk to her anymore. She says Susan makes her nervous. I don't know what's to become of her. Sometimes, late at night, I hear Susan crying. But she won't let me—" Suddenly she put a hand to her mouth. "Goodness! I didn't mean to say all that!" Her shoulders slumped, and she sighed heavily. "But I guess it's true. I wish someone could help me with her."

"Stay calm!" said Maybelle, lifting her forefinger as if she were about to holler *Chaaarrrge!* "Help is on the way."

Mrs. Pfenstermacher wiped at her nose. "What do you mean?" she sniffed.

Maybelle smiled slyly. "Let's just say that Susan has friends in high places."

Edna groaned slightly.

"What are you talking about?" asked Mrs. Pfenstermacher suspiciously.

Maybelle put on her best mysterious look. "Remember, when everything seems darkest, help can come from out of the blue. I have a suggestion: I think Susan needs to do more for others."

Mrs. Pfenstermacher snorted. "She's driving me crazy doing that now! She thinks it makes her more wonderful."

"Ah, but that's the problem," said Maybelle. "Her good deeds don't come from her heart. Now, does she have any relatives nearby?"

Mrs. Pfenstermacher hesitated. "Well, my mother lives just across the forest. But as I said, she doesn't talk to Susan anymore."

"That's all right. Now, let me see. Tomorrow is Saturday. Why don't you have Susan take a basket of fruit to her grandmother first thing in the morning?"

"What good will that do?"

"Just leave that to me," said Maybelle with a twinkle.

Mrs. Pfenstermacher scowled. "One of the woodcutters saw an imp in the woods yesterday."

"Don't worry. I'll be there."

Mrs. Pfenstermacher's scowl grew deeper. "Just who are you, anyway?"

Maybelle stuck her hand behind her and wiggled her fingers. "Here," she said, bringing her hand around front again. "My credentials."

"*Ribit*," said the frog she held in her hand.

"Oops! Wrong credential. Just a second."

Putting her hand behind her again, she closed her eyes and concentrated very hard. "Ah!" she said, when she felt a piece of paper materialize in her hand. "Here you go."

She handed the paper to Mrs. Pfenstermacher.

" 'Half off while supplies last'?" asked Mrs. Pfenstermacher, sounding puzzled.

"Sorry!" cried Maybelle. She reached behind her again, hoping desperately that Edna wouldn't feel it was time to step in yet. She concentrated harder than ever. "Here," she said after a moment when she feared her heart might stop. "*This* is what I meant to give you."

Mrs. Pfenstermacher took the paper, which had a gold seal at the bottom, and read aloud: " 'Be it known that Maybelle Clodnowski is hereby appointed my special emissary to deal with difficult children.' " Her eyes widened. "It's signed by the king!"

Maybelle sighed in relief. "I was hoping it would be. So, will you send Susan out with that basket of fruit tomorrow?"

"Well . . ." said Mrs. Pfenstermacher nervously.

"It's the only way," said Maybelle. "Trust me on this. I'm an expert in helping people."

Mrs. Pfenstermacher looked at the letter again. She rubbed the gold seal with her finger. "Oh, all right," she said at last.

"Excellent! I promise you'll see a big change in Susan after tomorrow."

"That would be lovely," said Mrs. Pfenster-macher. "Now, if you'll excuse me, I need to go lie down."

As Mrs. Pfenstermacher closed the door, Edna grabbed Maybelle by the elbow and dragged her away from the house. Neither of them noticed the little red creature who had been lurking in the bushes behind them.

Rubbing his hands together with impish delight, Zitzel raced into the forest to tell his boss what he had learned.

Chapter 6

Magic Apples

"What was *that* all about?" asked Edna sharply.

"I have a plan," said Maybelle.

"That's what I was afraid of. Well, you'd better tell me about it. What are you going to do?"

"Make a magic apple."

"A magic apple?" asked Edna in disbelief. She gave Maybelle a little push on the head, to get her feet back on the ground.

"Uh-huh," said Maybelle, struggling to stay down. "A *love* apple. I'm going to slip it into that basket of fruit Susan will be carrying."

Edna snorted. "Honestly, Maybelle, you are a simple thing."

"But, Edna, love conquers all."

"What's that got to do with Susan?"

"She's lonely. She has no friends. All that stuff about being perfect is because she doesn't feel loved. And since the best way to get love is to give it, I'm going to make her a love apple."

Edna tightened her mouth. "Those things are dangerous, Maybelle. They can have awful side effects. And stop floating!"

"Fiddledeedee," said Maybelle, bouncing a little as she struggled to make her feet connect with the ground. "What's wrong with love?"

"It makes people cuckoo! What would happen if *we* went around falling in love?"

Maybelle made a face. *"We* can't."

"Oh yes we can. But we don't. And you know the reason why."

Maybelle sighed. "Of course. *The Official Fairy Godmother Handbook,* page twelve, paragraph six: 'Any fairy godmother who falls in love shall lose her powers, be stripped of her wings, and be doomed to live as a mortal.' "

"Right!"

"That's kind of rough, isn't it?"

Edna tightened her lips and let her eyes get all squinty. "It maintains order," she said in a cold voice.

"Oh, phooey," said Maybelle. "Anyway, this apple isn't for us, it's for Susan."

"And just how are you planning to get her to eat it?"

"One bite will be enough."

"Well, how are you going to get her to take one bite?"

"I'll make it perfect."

"So?"

Maybelle smiled. "The apple will be perfect. Susan isn't. She won't be able to resist it!"

Edna began to smile too. "Why, Maybelle," she said. "There may be hope for you yet!"

Out in the forest Zozmagog was pacing back and forth in front of his cave, muttering to himself.

Zitzel followed close on his heels. "So, what are you gonna do, boss?" he asked eagerly.

"Quiet! I'm thinking! And watch out for my tail, you twit!"

"Sorry," said Zitzel, hopping backward.

He walked farther behind Zozmagog for about three minutes, but then began moving closer and closer again. Suddenly Zozmagog stopped dead in his tracks. "I've got it!"

"Ooof!" said Zitzel, running into him. "Got what?"

Zozmagog turned and gave his assistant a noogie. "Got what I'm going to do, you nitwit. Look, Maybelle's job is to humanize Susan, right?"

"Yeah."

"Well, we're going to do it for her."

Zitzel wrinkled his shiny red brow. "I don't get it."

"We'll make her cranky, nasty, mean, and generally rotten."

"Oh, now I get it. We're going to make her *really* human. You're a genius, boss! Now, how are we gonna do it?"

"With a 'perfect' apple. Now, where is that spell?"

"What spell?"

"I told you I was talking to myself!" said Zozmagog, giving Zitzel another noogie.

"Owww!" Zitzel rubbed his head. "Boy, you're awfully cranky for an imp, boss. We're supposed to be full of mischief. You know, merry pranks and all that?"

"Right," said Zozmagog. "I forgot. Jolly pranks. Ha ha ha ha ha. Have a laugh for me.

Now, where did I put— Oh, never mind. Wait here."

He went into the cave. Zitzel could hear a lot of scraping and thumping and muttering. After a few minutes Zozmagog emerged covered with dust and carrying a thick leather-bound book. It looked very old. Plunking himself down beneath a huge oak tree, he opened the book and began to flip through its pages.

"Not that. Not that. Not that. Ah, here it is! Oh, wonderful! *Perfect,* you might say. We'll make this and slip it into that basket the kid will be taking to her grandmother. She'll never be able to resist it."

"But what is it?" asked Zitzel.

Zozmagog smiled, and now he did look like a merry prankster. "A *crab* apple. Now get me these things: two dead toads, a pickled lizard's tongue, a gallon of vinegar, a stack of . . ."

The list went on and on. When it ended, Zitzel rubbed his hands together gleefully. "This is going to be fun!" he cried.

Then he scampered off to the secret place where imps keep their supplies.

Zozmagog went back into the cave to gloat.

"One more prank." He sneered. "One more

42

prank and that fairy godmother is done for good."

Then he threw back his head and laughed the laugh of the nasty.

While Zozmagog was in his cave, contemplating his revenge, Maybelle was rushing about gathering the ingredients she needed for *her* apple. Some of the things she had on hand already: the first sunbeam of a spring day, which she had been saving in a bottle for just such an occasion; the song of a meadowlark, a beautiful trill that she had caught in a handkerchief two summers earlier; the smell of bread just coming out of the oven, something that she carried with her always.

But the look of moonlight on still water, which was very hard to keep, she had to go out and fetch fresh. As she traveled, she also managed to get a bit of a mother's smile, a gurgle from a baby that had just discovered its toes, and the laughter from a family picnic on a summer evening. She caught the sound of church bells, the whisper of wind on the grass, the smell of laundry just brought in from hanging in the fresh air. She gathered the feel of a mother's lap, the safety of a father's embrace, and something that hung in the air between two very old people who were sitting in rockers on their front porch.

When she was ready with all these things and more, Maybelle flew to a cloud and began her conjuration.

At the same time, far below her, Zozmagog began to work on *his* apple. Deep in his cave, he poured together his ingredients and chanted:

> Handfuls of hatred,
> Gallons of greed,
> One rotten apple
> Will do my bad deed!

Up on her cloud, Maybelle delicately stirred together her ingredients, mixing them with sunshine and singing:

> Handfuls of giving
> Sent from above,
> This perfect apple
> Will fill her with love.

She stirred and mixed and sang and fixed, and finally she held up the apple, red and sparkling in the sunshine.

"There!" she cried triumphantly. "A perfect apple to do my good deed!"

"There!" cried Zozmagog, holding up his apple at the very same moment. "A rotten apple to do my bad deed!"

Then both of them began to laugh, Maybelle on her cloud and Zozmagog in his cave, one making a sound like wind chimes, the other a sound like stones grinding in the dark.

Clutching their apples, they hurried off to do their work.

Chapter 7

Into the Woods

Susan didn't really want to take a basket of fruit to her grandmother. But she knew that good girls always did as their mothers asked. So on Saturday morning she took the basket her mother gave her and headed toward the forest.

"Now, remember," said Mrs. Pfenstermacher, "don't talk to strangers while you're in the woods!" She paused, then added, "Unless you meet a little pudgy woman. Her you can talk to."

"Yes, Mother darling," said Susan, slightly puzzled by this odd pronouncement.

She kissed her mother and headed for the woods. On the way, she saw Heidi and Maria playing with their dolls. She thought it might be nice to stop for a while, but they never wanted to play with her. Besides, she told herself, perfect girls didn't stop to play when they had a job to do.

When she reached the edge of the forest she paused for a minute, wondering if there really were imps lurking inside, as the old woodcutter had said.

"Probably not," she decided. "Everyone knows he's not a very truthful old man."

Tightening her grip on her basket, she skipped into the forest, singing, "I'm perfect, so perfect, I'm as perfect as a perfect thing can be."

She hadn't gone far when she stopped to look around. "What a glorious morning!" she cried. "What a divine day. It's almost as perfect as I am!"

Suddenly a pudgy little woman appeared on the path ahead of her. Looking over her shoulder, the woman said something that sounded like "All right, all right, you don't have to push!"

Susan blinked, and for a moment she thought about running away. Then she remembered what her mother had said. Putting on a big smile, she stepped forward and asked politely, "Are you the pudgy little woman my mother told me about?"

The little woman looked slightly startled. "I suppose so," she said. Then she smiled, a wonderful smile that made Susan feel warm inside. "Actually, I'm your fairy godmother. My name is Maybelle."

The warm feeling vanished. Susan burst into laughter. "That's ridiculous. How could *I* have someone like *you* for a fairy godmother?"

Maybelle glanced behind her. Then she spread her hands, shrugged, and said, "Heaven works in mysterious ways."

Susan looked at Maybelle more carefully.

She was a pleasant-looking little woman, though not very carefully put together, what with her apron being so rumpled and the cloudy wisps of hair escaping all around the braid at the top of her head. Also, her slip was showing. Obviously she was crazy.

I'd better humor her, thought Susan, remembering a story her father had told her about a crazy villager. Out loud she said, "You poor dear. Why don't you sit down and rest?"

Looking bewildered, Maybelle sat on the log that Susan gestured toward.

"Now," said Susan, sounding very solemn, "tell me all about it. How did they start?"

"How did what start?" asked Maybelle.

"Why, the terrible troubles that have brought you to this sorry state."

Maybelle blinked. "What do you know about my troubles?"

"Nothing, except that it's obvious you have them. When did they begin?"

Maybelle scrinched her face into its thinking position. "Well," she said at last, "I guess it was about a hundred and fifty years ago."

"Oh, my!" gasped Susan. "This is worse than I thought!"

Maybelle nodded. "It is pretty bad when you think about it. It's been a long time."

"And what do you suppose caused these troubles?" asked Susan, her voice serious and sympathetic. She was sitting next to Maybelle now, thinking it would be nice if she could make the little woman sane again. She wondered if that was why her mother had sent her into the woods—so that she could work a miracle!

Maybelle shook her head. "I don't know."

Then, to Susan's alarm, she sighed heavily and lay down, resting her head in Susan's lap.

"You know," Maybelle said, settling in comfortably, "it's almost as if someone was out to get me."

"Oh! I see," said Susan, remembering an old man who used to wander around their town saying the same thing.

"For heaven's sake," muttered Edna Prim.

Making sure she was invisible, she stepped forward and poked Maybelle in the side.

Maybelle jumped and looked around, but didn't get the message.

Edna poked Maybelle again. Then she knelt by her ear and whispered, "Put the apple in the basket!"

Maybelle blinked. "I almost forgot!"

"Forgot what?" asked Susan.

"Uh . . . uh . . . I almost forgot that I'm not here to talk about my troubles. I'm here to talk about yours."

As she spoke, Maybelle jumped up and put her hand in her apron pocket, where the perfect apple was waiting.

"How can we talk about my troubles?" asked Susan primly. "I don't have any."

"You mean you're completely happy?"

"*Perfectly!*" said Susan, somewhat sharply.

"And there's nothing that bothers you?"

"Not a thing!"

"So everything is just the way you like it?"

"*Of course it is!*"

"That's wonderful," said Maybelle softly. "I'm glad things are going so well for you."

"It's not fair," said Susan, her voice grumpy

now. She crossed her arms and looked in the other direction.

Maybelle took advantage of the moment to slip the magic apple into Susan's basket. It sparkled enticingly. "What's not fair?" she asked gently.

"I work very hard at being good."

Maybelle smiled. "That's nice, dear. But it's not unfair."

"But nobody likes me!" shouted Susan.

"Ah. Now, *that's* not fair."

"I don't get it," Susan said bitterly. "I *try* to be nice. I *try* to be sweet. I *try* to be kind."

"Well, you certainly are trying," agreed Maybelle.

"But it doesn't do any good." Susan's shoulders slumped. "Maybe *I'm* no good."

No sooner had the words left her mouth than her eyes shot open and she sat straight up. "That's ridiculous. I'm perfect!"

"Is that important?"

"Certainly. If I'm perfect, people will have to like me."

"Well, *do* people like you?"

"No!"

Maybelle smiled. "Does that tell you anything?"

"Yeah. They don't know a good thing when they see it!" said Susan, crossing her arms and scowling. "They're all jealous anyway. I'm too good for them. But they act as if they're too good for me! They won't even play with me!"

"How can anyone be too good for anyone else?" said Maybelle softly.

Susan looked surprised. "What do you mean?"

"Oh, I've been studying you mortals for a long time, dear, and I have to tell you that you're more complicated than you think. You always seem to put on masks, as if you're afraid of what you are inside. My advice is to just be yourself and stop worrying about whether or not you're perfect."

"But I *am* perfect," replied Susan, a little desperately.

"You're a little young for it, aren't you?"

"I started early."

Maybelle sighed. "You've got more inside you than you're showing, Susan. Why don't you start to share it?"

Susan looked offended. "I always share!"

"You don't share your laughter," said Maybelle, grinning slyly. "In fact, I don't think you *can* laugh."

54

"Of course I can."

"Prove it."

Susan puckered up her face. "Ha."

Maybelle rolled her eyes.

"Ha-ha?" asked Susan.

"Pathetic," said Maybelle sadly.

"Ha-ha-*ha!*"

Maybelle just shook her head.

"Teach me!" demanded Susan.

Maybelle sighed. "You don't need to be *taught*, silly. The laughter is already there. You just have to let it out."

Susan made a face that looked a little like she had just swallowed a frog. Then she rolled her eyes back in her head, as if she was trying to see what was there. "Ha-ha-ha-ha-ha-ha!"

Maybelle giggled. "You sound like a drumroll."

Susan folded her hands in her lap and pursed her lips. "I was trying my best. Effort should always be rewarded."

"Well, try harder at not trying. That should be an effort for you."

"Huh?"

"Laugh!"

"Ha?"

"Laugh!"

"Hoo?"

"Laugh!" cried Maybelle. Standing up, she flung her arms wide, as if she was conducting a symphony. As she did she stepped backward, tripped over a stump, and tumbled to the ground.

Susan burst into peals of laughter.

"Now, *that's* not funny!" snapped Maybelle.

"It sure looked funny," gasped Susan. Quickly she put her hand to her mouth. "But you're right. It wasn't nice to laugh at your misfortune. Oh, no!"

"Well, it wasn't all *that* bad," said Maybelle, getting to her feet. She shook herself, and the dirt and leaves clinging to her dress disappeared in a shower of little sparks. Two twigs and a leaf remained stuck in her hair.

"I know it wasn't terrible," said Susan. "But it wasn't perfect, either. And if I'm not perfect—"

"People won't like me," finished Maybelle. She sighed. "Listen, Susan, the truth of it is, *no one* is perfect. Good grief, even fairy godmothers can make mistakes. But even though you're not perfect—"

"Hey!"

Maybelle sighed and started again. "Even if you weren't perfect, I would like you just fine."

"You would?" cried Susan in astonishment.

"Of course I would. I *do*."

Susan paused. "I like you too," she said at last, as if she was trying out the words to see how they sounded.

Maybelle looked as surprised as Susan had a moment earlier. "Really?" she asked.

Susan tightened her face as if thinking real hard. "Really!" she said at last. Then, as if she had said too much, she added quickly, "But I should go see my grandmother now."

Grabbing her basket, which now had Maybelle's love apple on top, Susan started down the path.

"Have a good time!" called Maybelle.

As she stood and watched Susan go, she was so excited it was all she could do to keep from floating.

"This is going to be just . . . lovely!" she whispered to herself.

Chapter 8

The Old Switcheroo

*F*arther along the same path Zozmagog sat clutching his magic crab apple, waiting impatiently (which was the only way he ever waited) for Susan.

Zitzel crouched in a bush on the other side of the path. His job was to create a distraction when Susan finally showed up. He was to do this by being very quiet until she appeared and then making a sudden movement. The main problem was that Zitzel hated being quiet and wanted to move all the time.

"Stop wiggling, you little git!" hissed Zozmagog, after he heard Zitzel shake his bush for the fifteenth time in five minutes.

"Jeez-o-Pete, boss," whined the little imp. "Gimme a break, will ya?"

Before Zozmagog could answer, Susan arrived, swinging her basket and singing, "She likes me, she likes me, she green-and-yellow likes me. She likes me, she—"

Zitzel shook the bush he was hiding in so hard that several leaves fell off.

Susan stopped in her tracks.

"Goodness, what was that?" She put a finger to her cheek and thought. "Oh!" she cried at last. "Perhaps it was a sweet little bunny. I want to see the fluffy thing."

Setting her basket on the path, she tiptoed carefully to the bush.

At the same time, Zitzel scooted backward into the forest.

From the other side of the path, Zozmagog moved swiftly and silently out of the bush where *he* was hiding. He snatched an apple from the top of Susan's basket and replaced it with the magic crab apple. Then he hurried back to his hiding place . . . completely unaware that the apple he had snatched was Maybelle's love apple.

Susan searched all around the bush without

finding any sign of a rabbit—or of Zitzel, for that matter.

"Oh, poobity-pobble," she said softly. It was one of her favorite curses. She went back to the path to get her basket. When she did, she noticed the apple resting on the very top.

It was remarkably beautiful. In fact, it was just about . . .

"Perfect!" said Susan. She looked around. No one was watching, at least as far as she could tell. "In fact, it's so perfect, it's as if it was made just for me," she said, not having any idea how accurate this statement really was.

"Of course," she continued, "if it was made for me, then it would be wrong for me *not* to take it. Besides, Granny would never want me to go hungry. The dear old thing would *want* me to eat this apple if I needed it."

And with that she took the apple from the top of the basket. Though it already sparkled in a stray ray of sunlight that had made its way through the leaves, she polished it on her dress for good measure.

Then she took a big bite.

A strange expression crossed Susan's face. Her eyes grew very wide and then narrowed. With a cry of disgust she flung the apple against the nearest tree so hard that it splattered into mush when it hit.

"Phooey!" she cried. "Why am I taking a basket to my grandmother anyway? I hate baskets. And I hate grandmothers. And Granny hates me, for that matter, the skinny old bat." She looked around. "Who designed this stupid forest anyway? It has too many trees! It's ugly. *Uglyuglyugly!*"

With that, Susan stamped off through the woods, roaring at the top of her lungs, stomping on mushrooms, and spitting at baby birds.

As soon as she was out of sight, Zitzel came rolling out from behind a tree. He was laughing so hard he couldn't stand up.

"Oh, boss," he gasped, "that was per . . . per . . . *perfect!*"

"Not bad, if I do say so myself," replied Zozmagog. He was still holding the apple he had taken from the basket. "In fact, I think that ought to finish Maybelle Clodnowski's career for good, Zitzel. At last, victory is ours!" Holding up the apple he had taken from the basket, he said, "Here's to apples!"

Then he took a big bite.

At once he began to choke.

"Boss!" cried Zitzel. "Boss, are you all right?"

Zozmagog was bent over double, unable to answer.

Zitzel began to pound him on the back.

Suddenly Zozmagog swallowed the chunk of apple that had been lodged in his throat. As he straightened up, his face began to twist itself into shapes and expressions it had not worn in over a century.

Without even looking at Zitzel, he began to run down the path. Ahead of him he saw Edna, who was just stepping out of the woods after having a conversation with Maybelle.

When Zozmagog saw the tall fairy godmother he stopped in his tracks.

"You!" he cried. "You are the most beautiful thing I have ever seen."

Edna turned toward him, then gasped in astonishment and horror.

"Oh, fair one, I think I love you!" cried Zozmagog. "No. Forget that. There's no 'think' about it. I *do* love you. I adore you. I worship the ground you walk on! Will you be my snookie-wudgums?"

With that, he rushed toward her.

With a shriek, Edna turned and ran deeper into the forest.

Zozmagog ran after her, shouting, "Kiss me, kiss me, kiss me, snookie, or I think that I shall die."

Trailing after them came Zitzel, crying, "Boss! Boss! Come back!"

Chapter 9

The Inner Brat

$\mathcal{D}r$. Derek Dekter was crossing the town square when Susan Pfenstermacher's mother came hurtling out of her house.

"Oh, Dr. Dekter, Dr. Dekter! I'm so glad you were passing by. Can you help us?"

Dr. Dekter was a tall man, heavyset, dressed all in black. His white beard was neatly trimmed. In fact, everything about him was neat and precise. In a severe voice he said, "Whether I can help you, Frau Pfenstermacher, depends entirely upon what is wrong, which you have so far failed to tell me."

"It's Susan. She's changed all of a sudden!"

Susan's father came stumbling out of the house. His eyes were wild, his face desperate.

"She's not cheerful and well behaved like she always was, Dr. Dekter."

"She's gotten mean!" added Mrs. Pfenstermacher.

"Nasty!" agreed Mr. Pfenstermacher.

"Rotten!" cried Mrs. Pfenstermacher.

"And she's started making bad puns!" moaned Mr. Pfenstermacher.

"Will you inspect her, Dr. Dekter?" asked Mrs. Pfenstermacher desperately.

The doctor shrugged. "It sounds like a simple case of puberty to me. But if you insist—"

"Oh, thank you, Dr. Dekter!" cried Mr. Pfenstermacher. He grabbed the doctor by the hand and began dragging him toward the house. Before they had gone three steps, Susan came leaping out the front door.

The index finger of her right hand was firmly planted in her nose.

"Dr. Dekter!" she cried. "Thank God you're here! My finger is stuck. It's stuck, I tell you— stuck, stuck, stuck, and I'm going to die! Save me, doctor. *Save me!*"

With her left hand she grabbed her right wrist and began to pull at it.

"Look at that!" she shrieked. "It will *never* come loose. And all I wanted to do was get out

that potato that I stuck up there last night. Oh, Doctor, I'm sinking fast. Help me. Please help me!"

With that, she threw herself to the ground and began to flop back and forth, screaming and making little choking noises. "Agh! Aaargh! Ack! Ack! Ack!" Gradually her voice grew softer and softer.

"The horror," she whispered. "The horror."

Then she lay stretched out straight on the ground, flat and unmoving.

She stayed that way for about three seconds. Then she lifted her head and said, "Being stuck-up was the death of me."

"All right, you've had your fun, Susan," said Dr. Dekter. "Stand up. I want to listen to your heart."

He took her by the wrist and tried to pull her to her feet.

"Watch it, frost fingers!" shouted Susan, yanking her hand free. She scrambled to her feet and began to dust herself off. As she did so, Dr. Dekter removed his stethoscope from the black bag that he always carried with him. No sooner had he put the ends of it into his ears than Susan grabbed the other end. Putting it to her mouth she shrieked, "Testing, testing, one, two, three! Doc, Doc, can you hear me?"

Dr. Dekter staggered backward and pulled the tubes from his ears. "Susan, stand still. I want to check your throat. Stick out your tongue, please."

"Gladly!"

She grabbed the corners of her mouth and pulled them as far apart as she could. Then she stuck her tongue out so far it looked as if it might come loose at the other end. Dr. Dekter bent forward to examine her throat. As soon as he got close, she snapped her mouth shut.

"Ah-ah-ah! Let's not get too personal, Doc. A girl's throat is private, you know."

"Susan, open your mouth!"

Susan clamped her mouth shut and shook her head.

"Susan, I want to take your temperature."

"Try it and you'll feel my temper, sir!"

"Now, Susan, don't you act like that."

"Can't help it, I've become a brat! I'm such a brat, I'm such a brat you won't believe."

"Susan, you are not a brat."

"Yes, I am, and that is that."

"Will you stop making those stupid rhymes?" roared Dr. Dekter.

Susan turned around and wiggled her butt at him. Then she began to run in circles, making rude noises and shouting, "What's for supper? Booger stew! Some for me and some for you!"

When Dr. Dekter tried to grab her, his stethoscope fell off.

"A snake!" cried Susan. Shrieking with joy, she jumped on the black tubes. Suddenly she gasped in dismay. "Oh, dear! It's not a snake after all. It's Dr. Dekter's stethoscope!" She picked it up and handed it to him. "Here's your ears, Doc. Stop by again sometime."

Then she went running into the house shrieking, "I hate bunnies! I hate bunnies! I want to bite their heads off!"

After she slammed the door, Susan's mother said desperately, "Can you correct her, Dr. Dekter?"

"No!"

"But what should we do?" asked Susan's father.

"If I were you," growled Dr. Dekter, "I would put her in a box and send her to Australia! Good day!"

With that he stomped away from the Pfenstermacher house.

The doctor hadn't gone more than fifty feet

when he spotted a plump little woman sitting on the edge of the town fountain, sobbing hysterically and wiping her eyes with the edge of her apron.

"Well, what's the matter with *you?*" he asked impatiently.

"Waaaaah!" replied Maybelle.

"Good heavens, woman, stop that horrible caterwauling and tell me what's wrong."

"I'm Susan's godmother."

"Ah, I see," said the doctor. "Well, if I were you, I'd be crying too."

"You don't understand," sniffed Maybelle. "I'm her *fairy* godmother."

"What in heaven's name are you talking about?"

"Well, for over a hundred and fifty years everything I've done has gone wrong. So Mr. Peters—he's my boss—he sent me to take care of Susan, because he figured I couldn't do too much harm to her, I guess. Only I did, because after I made the apple, *this* happened, and now Edna will have to step in and then I'll lose my wings and I don't know what I'm going to . . . to . . . to dooo!"

She began to wail again.

"Come, come," said Dr. Dekter gruffly. "It

can't be that bad. Now, let's start again. You say you're Susan's godmother?"

"Her *fairy* godmother," sniffled Maybelle.

"You mean, that's how she thinks of you," said Dr. Dekter reasonably.

"No, that's what I am! And I made a love apple to help her." She held up an apple. "Here, I found it on the path. She must have dropped it. You can see where she took a bite. But it didn't work. Somehow I created a m-m-m-monster!"

Before Dr. Dekter could answer, Edna shot into view. She was holding up the hem of her dress and running as fast as she could. "Help!" she cried. "Save me!"

Zozmagog was hot on her heels. "Wait for me, dear heart, morning sun, little dewdrop of joy. Wait for me!"

"Edna!" Maybelle cried in horror. "Oh, *now* what's happened?" She turned to Dr. Dekter. "Here," she said, thrusting the apple into his hand. "Take this."

Then she raced off after Edna and Zozmagog.

Dr. Dekter sat on the edge of the fountain, blinking in astonishment. He began tossing the apple up and down as he went over everything that had happened from the time Mr. and Mrs.

Pfenstermacher had stopped him. He looked back at the house. He looked down at where Maybelle had been sitting. He looked in the direction where everyone had run off. Finally he shrugged and absentmindedly took a bite of the apple.

Instantly his eyes grew wide.

"Wait!" he cried, springing to his feet. "Little pudgy woman, come back! I think I love you!"

He paused. "Love her? How can I love her? I just met her! Besides, she's so short!"

He shook his head. "What does time matter? What does short matter? What does pudge matter? *I love her!*"

And with that, Dr. Dekter raced off after Maybelle, Edna, and Zozmagog.

Chapter 10

Zozmagog's Secret

Edna Prim was running in circles around a big tree, and she had just about had it.

She had been horribly startled when the imp spotted her in the forest and began chasing her. But no mere imp was going to torment her like this. Stopping in her tracks, she turned around and drew herself up to her full height. Raising one hand, she snapped, "That will be about enough of *that!*"

It was a voice that could have stopped a bull elephant, much less a mere imp. Zozmagog stopped so fast he nearly fell over. Then he stood very still, staring up at her in astonishment.

"All right, just why are you chasing me?"

73

asked Edna in a tone that demanded he answer.

"Because I love you," Zozmagog moaned. "You are the sun and the moon and the stars. You are—"

"Oh, angel feathers. Cut the baloney, you little monster. Imps can't fall in love."

"*I* have," said Zozmagog. Then he tipped his head back and moaned hopelessly. "I'm in looooove with a wonderful woman."

"Oh, sit down," commanded Edna. "*Now!*"

Zozmagog sat. At that moment Zitzel came on the scene. When he saw what was going on, he hid behind a tree to listen. After all, it was possible the boss was working on some master prank. If he interrupted now, it could mean noogies for a week.

"All right, describe this *love*," said Edna, pronouncing the word "love" as if it tasted like mustard mixed with vinegar and thistles.

Zozmagog made his thinking face. "Well, my insides are all jumbled up." He put his hand on his chest. "And I have a burning sensation right here. My stomach is in a knot. Yet I feel all bubbly inside."

"That's not love, it's heartburn. You've been eating too much spicy food."

Zozmagog threw back his head and howled mournfully.

"Stop that!" said Edna. "It's disgusting."

"Well, it's not easy being an imp in love."

"Not easy? It's impossible! Magic can't create love out of nothing. And imps have no love. So that apple couldn't have affected you."

"But it did." Zozmagog sprang to his feet. "Kiss me, or I shall die!"

"*What?*"

"Kiss me, you gorgeous tower of femininity!"

He rushed toward Edna. She sidestepped him, and he ran into the tree.

He was too much in love to notice. Spinning around, he began to chase her again, crying, "Kiss me, kiss me, kiss me!"

They made another three or four circuits of the tree. Then Edna stopped, turned around, and rapped him sharply on the nose with her wand.

"Owwww!" cried Zozmagog. "Ow! Ow! Ow! What did you do that for?"

Grabbing his nose, he turned away from Edna and bent over, sobbing and moaning as if he was in blazing agony. Actually, his nose didn't hurt that much. But he was hoping he might get some sympathy.

He was barking up the wrong fairy godmother. Reaching forward, Edna grabbed his tail. "Straighten up!" she ordered, giving his tail a stiff tug.

It broke off in her hand.

She stared at the severed tail in horror. "Good heavens!" she shrieked. "What have I done?"

Zozmagog spun around. "Give me that!" he cried, snatching the tail back from her. If anything, he was even more horrified than she was. He stared at the tail for a moment, then threw himself to the ground and began to roll around, moaning and groaning. Finally he looked up and said, "If you tell Zitzel about this I'll never forgive you." He paused for a moment, then added. "Of course, I'll still *love* you. But I'll never forgive you."

"But how could this happen?" asked Edna, who was feeling as guilty as if she had stepped on a kitten. Suddenly her eyes widened. "Wait a minute. Look at me." She bent so that she was face-to-face with Zozmagog, who was desperately averting his eyes.

"Look at me!" she said again, in a voice that left no room for disobedience.

Zozmagog turned back and looked directly into her eyes.

"Aha!" said Edna.

He ducked his head. "All right," he said mournfully. "You've guessed it. I'm *not* an imp. When I was born, my fairy godmother delivered me to the wrong place."

"Impossible!" Edna snorted.

"Just because you think something is impossible doesn't mean it can't be true. Anyway, the imps that got me were thrilled. They loved teaching me to be rotten."

Edna took a deep breath. "Then what you really are . . ."

"Is a love-struck cherub," moaned Zozmagog.

Edna reached up. Snapping her fingers, she pulled a lace handkerchief from the air. She wet it with her tongue, then began to scrub at Zozmagog's cheek.

"Hey, watch it!" he said, trying to squirm away from her.

"It's true!" cried Edna, after she had cleaned off several layers of grub and grime. "You *are* a cherub!"

"I told you," said Zozmagog. "Anyway, those imps made my life so miserable that I vowed I would get revenge on the woman who did this to me."

"And who was that?" asked Edna.

"Maybelle Clodnowski."

Edna let out a heavy sigh. "Suddenly all of this makes sense." She sat down next to Zozmagog and put her arm around his shoulders. "You poor little cherub," she said sadly.

Zitzel was still watching from the bushes. "I think I'm gonna puke," he muttered, holding his stomach.

Suddenly Edna stood up. "Well, I'll take care of this," she said decisively. "Even if it does cost Maybelle her wings."

"Will you really?" asked Zozmagog.

Edna snorted again. "I haven't been Fairy Godmother of the Year for a hundred and forty-seven years in a row for nothing, Buster."

Zozmagog sighed. "You're wonderful. I love you so much. What's your name?"

In the bushes, Zitzel was sticking his finger in his throat and pretending to vomit.

"You know, I never wanted to be bad," continued Zozmagog in a dreamy voice. "It was just the way they raised me. Naughtiness was the only thing I knew, until I met you." Turning toward Edna, looking directly into her eyes, he said sincerely, "I was lonelier than you can ever know. My heart hurt so much that I finally put a wall around it. But when I saw you today, somehow that wall just crumbled."

A little tear trickled down his cheek.

Edna reached out to brush the tear away. As she did, she felt a strange fluttering in her chest. Her eyes widened.

"Oh, no!" she whispered in horror. "Not that! I can't let *that* happen! Listen, you—"

"My name is Zozmagog."

"Listen, Zozmagog. I *need* a wall around my heart. It saves me from chaos. If that wall ever starts to crack, my career as a fairy godmother will be over. Please—don't knock on a door that I don't dare answer. Please." She took a deep breath, then said fiercely, "I want to help you. You've been terribly wronged, and it is my duty to give you assistance. But that's all. A fairy godmother must *never* fall in love."

Zozmagog sighed heavily.

"Look," said Edna primly. "We'll find a cure for the effects of that apple. Then you'll be just fine."

"But I don't want to be cured!" cried Zozmagog. Suddenly he sat up straight, and his eyes went wide. "Wait a minute! What about that poor girl who got *my* apple? I feel awful about that."

Edna looked at him nervously. "What, exactly, are you talking about?"

Quickly Zozmagog explained to her about the crab apple he had made for Susan.

"Well, that certainly does complicate things," said Edna disapprovingly. "But with your help, I'm sure I can disenchant the poor girl."

"It won't be easy," said Zozmagog. "The spell can only be broken one way. She has to tell someone she loves them."

Edna gasped. "But if she's so cranky and crabby—"

"Exactly," said Zozmagog glumly. "And that's not the worst of it."

"There's *more?*" asked Edna sharply.

Zozmagog looked away, embarrassed.

"Zozmagog," said Edna, "what have you done?"

The cherub in disguise sighed. "Susan is contagious. Any kid who comes into close contact with her is going to catch the spell and start acting in the same incredibly bratty way."

"Gracious!" cried Edna. "You *were* nasty, weren't you? I'll have to see that spell, and quick! Come on!"

Grabbing Zozmagog by the hand, she pulled him to his feet.

Zozmagog started to lead her in the direction of the cave.

Zitzel was about to follow when someone grabbed him from behind.

Chapter 11

Susan's Rampage

Gotcha!" cried Susan happily. "Gotcha, gotcha, gotcha!"

"Let go!" cried Zitzel, squirming wildly.

Susan just laughed.

"What do you want?" asked Zitzel, still squirming. He was surprised at how strong she was.

"What do I want? I want to cause trouble! I want to bug people! I want to be rude, nasty, and generally socially unacceptable."

Zitzel began to smile.

Maybe things weren't so bad after all.

"Let go of me, and I can help you!" he said.

Susan let go. Then she gave him a noogie. "I'll tell you what I like," she said. "I like spittin', cussin', and fightin'."

"Hey, me too!" said Zitzel.

"Man, I can't believe all the time I wasted," growled Susan as she whacked Zitzel on the head. "Years of perfect sweetness! Yetch! I never got out of my seat unless I was supposed to. I never took off my shoes until it was time for bed. Heck, I never even picked my nose in public! I tell you, it is time for this girl to cut loose."

"I agree," said Zitzel, rubbing his hands together. "What shall we do first?"

"Let's beat each other up!" cried Susan. With that, she launched herself at Zitzel and began to pound him on the head.

"Ow! Ow! Ow!" he cried. "Stop that, will ya? I'm on your side."

"You're not on my side, you're underneath me!" shouted Susan as she pinned the little imp to the ground. She began flicking his ears, singing "Flickety, flickety, bop-bop-bop!" Then she grabbed them and pulled them out sideways. "Man!" she cried. "These are big enough to be wings!"

Before Zitzel could get loose, Gustav happened along. Susan jumped up and ran to him. "Hey, Gustav!" she cried, grabbing him by the shoulders and breathing in his face. "Let's fight!"

Gustav looked totally astonished. "Susan, is that you?"

"Sure is, you little slimeball," she said as she punched him on the shoulder.

Gustav stood stock still for a moment. Suddenly his mouth began to twitch. His eyes got wide and then very narrow.

"I hate everything!" he shouted.

"All right!" cried Susan. "That's the spirit!"

"Shut up!" replied Gustav. "You make me sick."

Susan laughed. "So what's new? I always made you sick, liver brain."

Then she hit him on the head.

Gustav began chasing her. They went barreling toward the town. As they did, they met Maria. Susan stopped long enough to grab one of Maria's pigtails. "Hey, Maria!" she cried, running in circles and pulling Maria with her. "You must be built upside down, because your nose runs and your feet smell!"

Maria gasped in astonishment. "Susan, what are you—"

She broke off in mid-sentence. Her eyes got

wide and then very narrow. Then she slapped Susan.

Susan slapped her back.

Soon the two girls were having a slap fight. *Slap! Slap! Slapitty-slap-bop!*

"Owwww!" cried Maria.

"Get over it, Toots!" shouted Susan.

Maria didn't answer. Instead, she began to growl as she came racing at Susan.

The yelling and screaming had brought Heidi and Friedrich running from their house.

"Stop it! Stop it!" cried Heidi.

"Aw, let them work it out themselves," said Friedrich, who thought the fight was very funny.

Suddenly Gustav jumped on his back. "Hey, Friedrich!" he cried. "Wanna wrestle?"

Actually, Friedrich and Gustav wrestled all the time. But when Gustav grabbed him now, Friedrich's face began to twitch. His eyes got narrow and then very wide. He wiggled free of Gustav's grasp.

He stood shaking and trembling for a moment. Then he straightened up. Sounding exactly like Susan used to, he said, "Of course I don't want to wrestle with you little hooligans.

Fighting is not a proper activity for a young gentleman. You should all be ashamed."

"Great bonging bells!" cried Zitzel, who was swinging on the ends of Maria's braids. "He must have been so crabby to begin with that the spell drove him right through to the other side. He's been double-crabbed, and he turned out nice! What a catastrophe!"

Before Zitzel could decide what to do, Gustav came charging over to fight with him instead.

Friedrich went running off, shouting, "Mommy, Mommy! Teacher, teacher! The children are being wicked, the children are being wicked. Save me, Mommy. Save me!"

At the same time Heidi grabbed Susan and pulled her away from Maria. "Stop fighting!" she cried.

"Leave me alone, pukeface!" roared Susan, breathing the words right into Heidi's face.

Heidi blinked. Her eyes went wide, then got very narrow. Her lip curled in a sneer. She grabbed Susan's hair and started to pull. "I've had it with you, you disgusting little china doll!" she shouted. "You've made me sick to my stomach for as long as I've known you."

Susan squirmed away from her and ran off

chanting, "Naughty girls and little pink pigs, Heidi and Maria are wearing wigs."

The commotion brought out Ludwig, who was soon infected as well. Helga showed up a moment later—and a moment after that, she was screaming and hitting too.

Before long there was a battle going on at the edge of town unlike anything anyone had ever seen. Every kid in Grindersnog had been attracted by the shouts and screams. Within seconds of reaching the fight, each newcomer was infected by the spell. Children who had been rambunctious but basically decent all their lives were screeching, swearing, and throwing punches left and right.

It was about then that Edna and Zozmagog showed up.

"Oh, no!" cried Edna. "We're not a moment too soon!"

"I'd say we're about ten minutes too late," said Zozmagog nervously. Then he added in surprise, "Zitzel, what are you doing here?"

Zitzel, who had risen briefly to the top of the writhing mass of brawling children, shouted, "Hi, boss! Just like the old days, huh?"

"Edna, my shimmering ray of sunlight, you'd better do something quickly!" said Zozmagog.

Edna took a deep breath. "Well, this won't cure them, but it will slow things down." Raising her wand, she waved it at the crowd of kids and chanted, *"Imminny, Bimminny, Arphaz ig Nantio!"*

Nothing happened.

Astonished, Edna shook the wand and tried again. *"Imminny, Bimminny, Arphaz ig Nantio!"*

Again nothing happened—at least, nothing magical. But at that moment the townspeople began to arrive. When the first woman to show up saw Edna shaking her wand at the children she began to scream, "A witch! A witch!"

"I told you there were demons in the forest!" shouted the woodcutter who had spotted Zitzel two days earlier.

Edna blinked in astonishment, then drew herself up to her full height. But before she could announce that she was a fairy godmother, not a witch, Susan shouted, "Grown-ups! Head for the hills!"

The kids all turned and blew raspberries at their parents. Then they scattered and ran. The grown-ups went chasing after them, leaving Edna and Zozmagog standing alone at the edge of the village.

"What happened?" asked Zozmagog. "How come you couldn't stop the fight?"

"I've lost my powers!" cried Edna in despair.

Chapter 12

Farewell to Heaven

Maybelle and Dr. Dekter were walking through the forest, talking quietly.

"So you really *are* a fairy godmother?" asked Dr. Dekter.

He was having a hard time accepting the idea, since they had never taught him anything about fairy godmothers in medical school.

"I certainly am!" replied Maybelle. "And the reason you fell in love with me was because you took a bite of that love apple I made to help Susan. Only I can't figure out why it made Susan so crabby."

"But why aren't I in love with you now?" asked Dr. Dekter.

"Because the darn thing wore off!" said Maybelle in disgust. "I blew it—just like I've blown everything else I tried to do for the last hundred and fifty-three years. I am a total failure, the worst fairy godmother in the entire world!"

Dr. Dekter put his hand on her shoulder. "Now, now, Maybelle. It can't be all that bad."

"Oh, no?" she cried. "How would *you* like to lose your wings and your wand?"

Dr. Dekter frowned. "Ah," he said sympathetically. "I see what you mean. I think . . ." He paused, looked up, and then said nervously, "What in heaven's name is going on there?"

In the distance they could hear a great shouting and commotion.

"I don't know," said Maybelle. "But I'm afraid maybe we should go find out."

They hurried toward the edge of the forest. Just as they reached it a herd of screaming, shouting children went thundering by.

"Wait!" cried Dr. Dekter.

No one stopped. However they did all turn and stick out their tongues.

Before Maybelle could ask what was going on, a mob of adults came racing toward them, shouting, "Come back! Come back!" Some of them sounded worried. Others sounded angry.

"What's going on?" cried Maybelle.

No one answered. They were too intent on catching the children.

"I think we'd better follow them," said Maybelle.

"Who's that?" said Dr. Dekter, pointing in the other direction.

Edna and Zozmagog were sitting beside the road. "I don't understand," said the cherub. "How could you lose your powers?"

"It means I've fallen in love," Edna said through clenched teeth.

"Wonderful!" cried Zozmagog. "I mean, that's too bad. I mean, great! I mean . . . is it with *me*, pookie?"

"It must be!"

"Oh, joy! Oh, rapture! Oh, heavenly bliss! Oh, Edna, my little kumquat, my gleaming star in the firmament, perfection on wings. Divine Edna, at last my life is complete!"

"Oh, shut up! I have to think."

But before she could think a single thought, Maybelle came huffing up, crying, "Edna! Edna! Oh, Edna, I blew it again."

"I am well aware of that," said Edna sharply.

"You might as well step in and fix things,"

said Maybelle sorrowfully. "I'm bound to get kicked out after this mess."

Edna sighed. "Maybelle, I can't fix a thing."

"Why not?"

"I've lost my powers."

Maybelle's eyes grew wide with astonishment. "What? *How?*"

"Guess," said Edna, her voice dripping with disgust.

Maybelle thought for a moment, then cried, "You're kidding! *You* fell in love?" She sounded astonished, delighted, and horrified all at once.

"Yes, I did," said Edna. "And you needn't look so surprised."

"Who's the lucky man?"

Edna gestured to Zozmagog, who was sitting next to her.

Maybelle, who had been so focused on her own troubles that she hadn't really taken a look at Edna's companion, was now more astonished than ever. She looked at Zozmagog for a moment, then motioned frantically for Edna to come close so she could speak to her in private.

When Edna obliged, Maybelle stretched up

and whispered into her ear, "Edna, do you—uh, do you know exactly what he is?"

"Yes, I know what he is!" said Edna sharply. "He's a cherub, believe it or not. And most of his troubles are due to you."

Maybelle rolled her eyes. "That figures. Aren't everyone's?"

"You delivered him to the wrong place when he was a baby," said Edna. "It ruined his life."

Maybelle turned pale. "Are you serious?"

"She most certainly is," said Zozmagog. "Look, here's proof. I've saved it all these years." Reaching into whatever place it is that imps and cherubs store their belongings, he pulled out a piece of cloth with a paper tag attached to it.

"What's that?" asked Edna.

"My diaper and address tag!" said Zozmagog.

Maybelle snatched it from him. "Let me see that!"

She studied the items carefully, then said, "I delivered him to exactly where this says. I remember that trip very well. It wasn't easy."

"Let *me* see," said Edna. She took the diaper and tag from Maybelle. "Well, it's misaddressed," she said sharply.

She blinked and looked at the tag again. Her

eyes grew wide, and the color drained from her cheeks until she was even paler than Maybelle. "I can't believe it!" she wailed. "That's *my* handwriting! I'm the one who caused it!"

"There, there, dear," said Maybelle, reaching up to pat Edna on the shoulder. "None of us are perfect."

Zozmagog rushed to Edna's side. "Don't cry, dear heart. It's perfectly all right. After all, without that mistake, I might never have come to know you. I would have lived in the darkness forever, gone my entire life without ever walking in the sunshine."

"Holy Moses," said Maybelle. "He really does have a case on you."

Edna sighed. "He certainly does. But it's only because of that foolish love apple of yours."

Maybelle smiled. "Edna, I've got news for you. That love apple doesn't work."

"What?"

"Ask him," she said, gesturing toward Dr. Dekter.

"She's telling the truth," said the doctor. "Half an hour ago I was crazy about Maybelle. But it wore off."

"It's the story of my life," muttered Maybelle.

Edna blinked. "But if the apple doesn't work—"

"Then this is for real!" cried Zozmagog. "Darling, how wonderful!"

"Oh, be quiet!" snapped Edna. "Don't you realize we won't be welcome anywhere now, above *or* below?" She sighed. "Oh, I will miss heaven."

"What's it like?" asked Zozmagog. "I never got to see it, you know."

"It's . . . it's . . . well, it's *heavenly*," said Edna.

"It sure is," said Maybelle. "We've got choirs of angels and troops of clowns. Music, light, and laughter all day long. Nectar dripping right out of the vine. And the dancing! Oh, I do love dancing on those golden streets of ours."

She fluttered into the air and began to do a little polka.

"And the pearly gates," sighed Edna. "You can see them shining in the dark no matter where you are." She sniffed sadly. "I will miss it up there, Maybelle."

Zozmagog sighed. "I can't let you give up all that for me, my darling little pookie-kumquat."

"I don't have any choice," said Edna. "Besides, you should have been there to begin with, and it's my fault you're not." Straightening her shoulders, she said, "We'll just have to make a little bit of heaven here on earth."

"Boy," Maybelle muttered to Dr. Dekter. "She's as gone as he is."

"Yes," said the doctor. "And it's all very sweet. But you've got another problem right now."

"Like what?"

"Like a village full of angry parents!" he said, pointing toward the forest.

Even as he spoke, most of the population of the village came pouring out of the forest. The parents had their children firmly in tow, carrying them over their shoulders or pulling them along by their ears. The children were screaming and squalling, kicking and shouting.

"Let me go!" screeched Susan. *"Let me go!"*

"Look!" cried a woman at the front of the crowd. "There she is!"

She was pointing at Edna.

"I saw her waving a wand over the children," continued the woman. "She's the witch who caused all this!"

"Witch?" said Edna in disbelief.

"And that other woman is her helper!"

shouted Susan's mother. "They came to my house yesterday and persuaded me to send Susan into the woods. That's when she changed. They must have cast an evil spell on her!"

"Evil spell?" asked Maybelle in astonishment.

"There's only one way to break a witch's spell!" shouted one of the men. "Burn her!"

The villagers took up the cry. "Burn them! Burn the witches!"

Chapter 13

Out of the Blue

"Edna!" cried Maybelle. "Do something!"

"I can't do anything," said Edna, and for the first time Maybelle heard fear in her voice. "I have no powers. *You* do something."

"But . . ." Maybelle took a deep breath. "Oh, all right. Here goes nothing." Lifting her wand, she waved it at the crowd and shouted, *"Zitzenspratz!"*

Immediately everything went dark.

Edna sighed. "For heaven's sake, Maybelle, turn on the lights."

"Sorry. *Brechensprech!*"

Lightning crackled all around them. Horrendous bursts of thunder shook the sky. The darkness remained.

"Maybelle," said Edna quietly, "that's very exciting, but it's not going to help. In fact it will probably make things worse."

"I know, I know!" said Maybelle desperately. Waving her wand, she shouted, "Cut!"

Instantly the thunder and lightning stopped. The light came back, and everyone could see again.

"Oh, Lordy!" cried Zozmagog. "I know what the problem is!" Snatching Edna's wand, he handed it to Maybelle. "Here," he said. "Use this one!"

He was too late. Several of the men had raced forward and grabbed the two women.

"Leave them alone!" said Dr. Dekter angrily.

"Stay out of this, old man," shouted one of the villagers. "Now, witch, prepare to meet your Maker!"

"Actually, I already have," said Maybelle. "He's quite nice. Frankly, I don't think he would approve of this."

"Kindly take your hands off me," said Edna in frosty tones to the man who held her. "I am *not* a witch!"

"Oh?" he sneered. "Then what are you?"

"A fairy godmother!"

The men burst into laughter. "And I suppose

this is just a sweet little cherub," said one of them, gesturing at Zozmagog.

"As a matter of fact, that's exactly what he is," said Edna fiercely.

The men laughed harder than ever.

"This is *not* funny!" said Edna.

"I'll say it's not!" shouted one of the women, who was struggling to hold on to a screaming, shouting little girl. "What have you done to these children?"

"Bewitched them!" shouted another woman. "That's what they've done! Bewitched them!"

"Burn them!" roared the crowd. "Burn the witches!"

"No!" cried Susan.

"Susan!" hissed Mrs. Pfenstermacher. "Be quiet."

"I won't!"

"Take Susan away," said one of the men. "Take them all away. What we have to do now is not for children's eyes."

Susan squirmed free of her mother's grasp and ran to stand in front of Maybelle. "Don't you touch her!" she cried. "They're telling the truth. She *is* a fairy godmother. She's *my* fairy godmother!"

"Susan!" cried Mr. Pfenstermacher. "Come

away from there. That woman is dangerous! She might . . . might . . . turn you into a frog!"

"Hey," said Maybelle. "No fair bringing up old mistakes."

Several of the men began to advance on her, muttering menacingly.

"I'm warning you," said Susan. "Don't touch this woman! She's the only person who has ever liked me. And I . . . I . . . I love her!"

The world seemed to hold its breath. There was a moment of deep and mysterious silence. Then an enormous crack of thunder sounded overhead.

Susan sighed and collapsed in a heap at Maybelle's feet.

At the same time the other children stopped squirming and struggling.

A sense of peace seemed to settle over the villagers.

"Susan did it!" cried Edna. "She broke the spell. Congratulations, Maybelle!"

Susan shook her head and sat up. "What happened?" she asked, sounding groggy.

The townspeople were all asking pretty much the same thing, shouting, "What happened? What's going on?"

"Make way, make way!" cried a stern voice.

It was the blind beggar to whom Susan had given a coin the day before. "Be quiet," he said, pushing his way to the front of the crowd. "All of you."

He spoke softly now, but his voice held a strength and a power that immediately calmed the crowd. Their shouts grew softer, turning to mutters, then fading to silence.

The beggar turned to Susan. "Well done, young lady!" he said. "I didn't think you had it in you."

"Who are you?" asked Susan, staggering to her feet.

"My name is Mr. Peters," said the beggar, pulling back his hood and taking off his dark spectacles.

"Well, I never!" said Maybelle in astonishment. "Look at that, Edna!"

"I decided to watch you up close this time, Maybelle," said Mr. Peters. "You made some awful blunders."

"Boy, you can say that again, boss. Well, we might as well get it over with. Take my wings. Break my wand. Tarnish my halo!" She sighed. "There's nothing worse than a failed fairy godmother."

"But, Maybelle, you're no failure. You said

106

it yourself: Susan needed to learn to love. It was your open heart that brought out that love. That's the most important thing a fairy godmother could ever do. Failure? Maybelle, you're a smashing success!"

Maybelle blinked in astonishment. "Love, huh? Gee, that's pretty classy."

"It beats the heck out of magic apples," said Mr. Peters.

Edna, who was standing behind Maybelle, began to sniffle.

Maybelle turned around. "Why, Edna," she said, "what's the matter?"

"I'm so embarrassed!" wailed the tall fairy godmother. "Mr. Peters has seen what I've done!"

"What did you do?" asked Maybelle, genuinely puzzled.

"I fell in love!"

"Oh, *that*," said Maybelle, waving her hand as if shaking something away. "You should never be embarrassed about loving someone."

Mr. Peters nodded. "Well put, Maybelle. She's right, Edna. You mustn't be embarrassed about loving someone."

"But the rules . . ." Edna sniffed.

"Are made to be broken," said Mr. Peters.

"As in this case. The being you fell in love with is not a human but an immortal. Therefore, you can still live in the blue."

"Wonderful!" said Maybelle.

"What about Zozmagog?" asked Edna, putting a protective hand on his shoulder.

Mr. Peters smiled. "He comes, too. But I'll warn you, he's going to have to earn his way."

"How can I do that?" asked Zozmagog.

"I want you and Edna to start a school to train fairy godmothers. You should be very useful, Zozmagog; you can teach the trainees about some of the dirty tricks they can expect to face from imps." He stooped to pick up Maybelle's wand. "Tricks like *sabotaged* magic wands."

"Why, you little devil!" said Maybelle.

Out of habit, Zozmagog glanced around, looking for someone else to blame. When he realized that wasn't possible, he said softly, "Sorry about that, Maybelle."

"Now," said Mr. Peters, "I think it's time we headed for home."

"Not yet," said Edna. "There's one more thing, and I want to do it now, before we go." Turning to Maybelle, Edna lifted the Fairy Godmother of the Year medallion from around her own neck. "Here, Maybelle," she said gently. "I think you should have this."

"The Fairy Godmother of the Year award! Oh, no, Edna. I couldn't—"

"Take it, Maybelle," said Mr. Peters gently. "You've earned it."

"Gosh," said Maybelle, as Edna placed the medallion around her neck.

"Oh, Maybelle!" cried Susan. "I am so happy for you!" She threw her arms around Maybelle and gave her a hug. "Only . . . will I ever see you again?"

Maybelle smiled sadly. "I don't think so, dear. After all, you don't really need me anymore."

"But . . ."

"But there's one thing you need to know. I really *do* like you. A lot! And I'll be watching over you."

Susan smiled.

"Come along, Maybelle," said Mr. Peters. "It's time for us to be going."

"Hey, what about me!" cried Zitzel.

"Can he come with us?" asked Zozmagog.

"Are you kidding?" cried Zitzel. "I'd be bored silly. And I'm silly enough as it is."

"Can he stay with us?" asked Susan, turning to her mother. "He's kind of cute."

"Oh, Susan, really, I don't think—"

"But, Mother," said Susan, "charity begins at home."

"I don't eat much," added Zitzel.

"But think of all the trouble!" said Mr. Pfenstermacher.

"I prefer mischief to trouble," said Zitzel, trying to look innocent. "Besides, I would protect the people I lived with."

"Is that true?" asked Mrs. Pfenstermacher.

"Absolutely," said Mr. Peters. "He would guard you against all sorts of goblins and ghoulies. Things might be a little . . . lively . . . at times. But you wouldn't have to worry about major problems."

"Besides," said Susan with a smile, "think of what a bad influence he would be on me!"

Mr. and Mrs. Pfenstermacher laughed. "All right, dear," said her father. "He can stay!"

The children all began to cheer.

"That was well done, Susan," said Maybelle. She stretched up and gave her a kiss on the forehead. "That's for luck," she whispered. Then she went to stand with Mr. Peters, Edna, and Zozmagog.

Mr. Peters made a gesture, and all four of them disappeared in a little puff of white smoke.

The smell of new hay and cinnamon lingered behind them, mingled with just a trace of beer and peppermint.

"Well," said Mr. Pfenstermacher, "that was the most amazing thing I've ever seen. Are you all right, Susan?"

"I never felt better in my life," said Susan, running to her parents and giving them each a hug.

"Me too!" cried Gustav.

"And me!" cried Helga and Ludwig and Friedrich.

"Well," said Mrs. Pfenstermacher, "I guess they really were what they claimed to be."

"Not exactly," said Dr. Dekter.

"What do you mean?" asked Susan.

Dr. Dekter smiled. "Maybelle told me she was the world's worst fairy godmother. But if you ask me, she was the world's best."

"Naturally," said Susan. "What other kind would I have?"

And she said it with such a charming laugh that no one wanted to slap her.

About the Author and the Illustrator

BRUCE COVILLE was born in Syracuse, New York. He grew up in a rural area north of the city, around the corner from his grandparents' dairy farm. In the years before he was able to make his living full-time as a writer, Bruce was, among other things, a gravedigger, a toymaker, a magazine editor, and a door-to-door salesman. He loves reading, musical theater, and being outdoors.

In addition to more than fifty books for young readers, Bruce has written poems, plays, short stories, newspaper articles, thousands of letters, and several years' worth of journal entries. Like his novel *The Dragonslayers*, *The World's Worst Fairy Godmother* is based on one of Bruce's musical plays.

Some of Bruce's best-known books are *My Teacher Is an Alien*, *Goblins in the Castle*, and *Aliens Ate My Homework*.

KATHERINE COVILLE is a self-taught artist known for her ability to combine finely detailed drawings with a deliciously wacky sense of humor. She is also a toymaker, specializing in creatures hitherto unseen on this planet. Her other collaborations with Bruce Coville include *The Monster's Ring*, *The Foolish Giant*, *Sarah's Unicorn*, *Goblins in the Castle*, *Aliens Ate My Homework*, and the *Space Brat* series.

The Covilles live in an old brick house in Syracuse, NY, along with their youngest child, three bad cats, and a very bouncy dog named Thor.